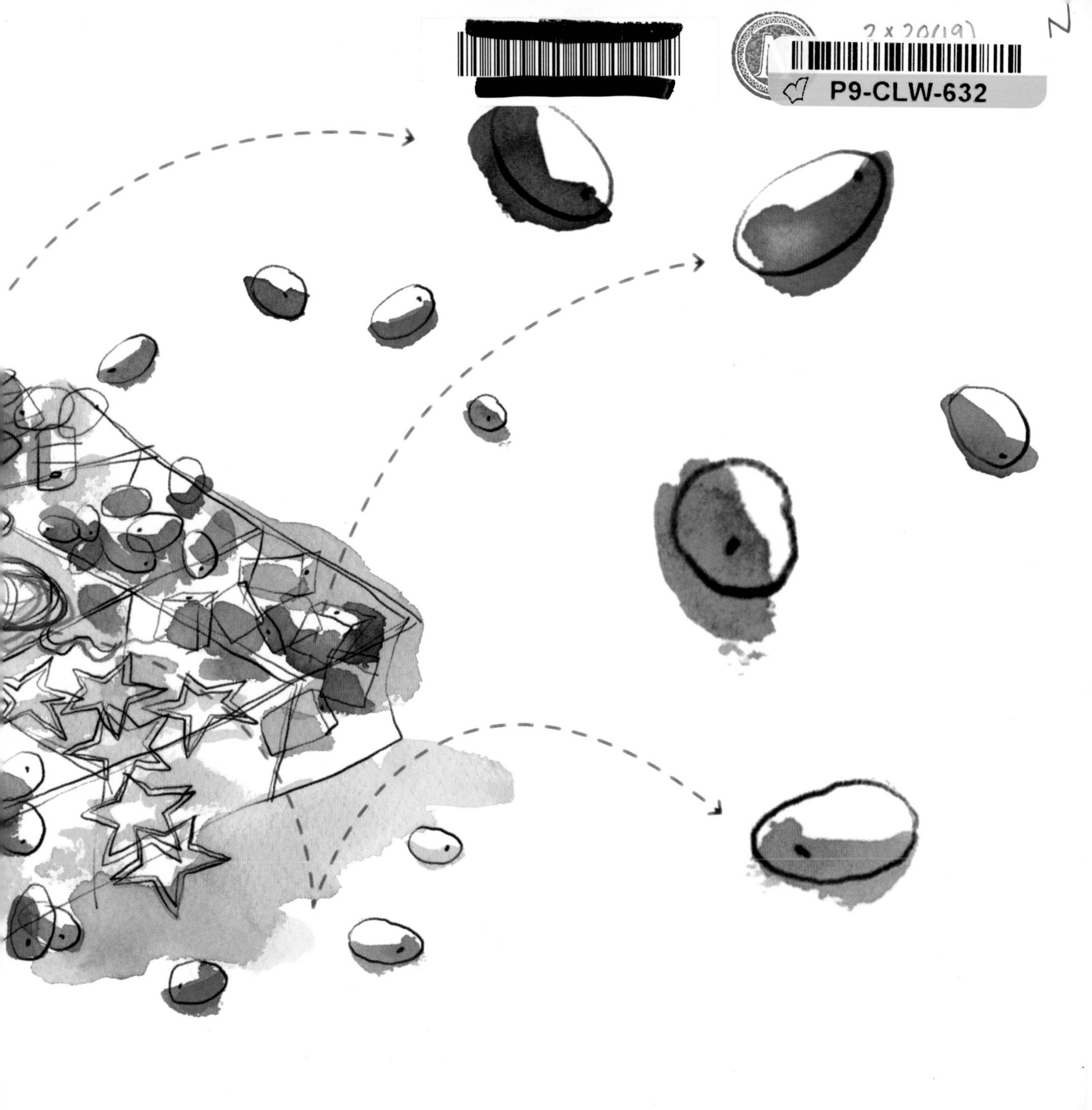

Emma's Gems

To Albert Moreau for planting the seed of this story, and to my father for all the love he gives Emma. – A. R.

To Carmelle, in memory of the good times we shared. – L. F.

Peanut Butter Press, 9-1060 Dakota Street, Winnipeg, MB R2N 1P2 · www.peanutbutterpress.ca

Translation by Anne Renaud
Design of the English-language version by Jason Doll, Animation Dog

Printed and bound in China by Midas Printing International Limited

10 9 8 7 6 5 4 3 2 1

Library and Archives Canada Cataloguing in Publication

Renaud, Anne, 1957-
[Pierres d'Emma. English]
Emma's gems / story and translation by Anne Renaud ; illustrations by Leanne Franson.

Translation of: Les pierres d'Emma.
ISBN 978-1-927735-65-7 (hardcover)

I. Franson, Leanne, illustrator II. Title. III. Title: Pierres d'Emma. English.

PS8635.E51P5313 2019 jC843'.6 C2018-904618-X

Emma's Gems

Story and translation by Anne Renaud
Illustrations by Leanne Franson

Grandpa Phil does not have to speak or sneeze or laugh for Emma to know he is near.

It is the familiar jingle-jangle of the coins in his pockets that always sounds his presence.

Emma wants to be just like Grandpa Phil,
so she carries coins in her pockets and makes
them chime by hopping around like a kangaroo.

Emma is always in a good mood when her grandfather comes to visit. But not today.

Today, Emma is a grump. Mother made her share her puzzles with her brother, Zachary, and Emma does not like sharing anything with anyone.

"Your mom tells me you're in a grizzly mood," says Grandpa Phil. "Why don't we take a walk around the neighbourhood. It might make you feel better."

So Emma and her grandfather set out together.

When Emma and Grandpa Phil reach the grocery store, they notice a man in tattered clothing and worn-out shoes sitting on the ground.

As they near him, Grandpa Phil slips his hand into his pocket. Then he bends down in front of the sad-looking man and places coins in his palm. "I think you may have dropped these," Grandpa Phil says softly.

Next, Emma watches her grandfather take a small stone from his right pocket and drop it into his left.

Then the two continue on their way.

When Emma and Grandpa Phil reach the park, they sit on a bench and giggle at the squirrels scampering in the trees.

Just as they are about to move on, Grandpa Phil kneels down and gently turns over a beetle that is on its back, struggling to right itself.

"There you go, little fellow," he says as he sets the beetle back onto its feet.

Next, Emma watches her grandfather take another small stone from his right pocket and drop it into his left.

Then the two continue on their way.

When Emma and Grandpa Phil reach the playground, they play hide-and-seek in the maze of tunnels. Then they leave their handprints and footprints in the giant sandbox.

Just as they are about to move on, Grandpa Phil picks up the empty bottles and cans that litter the ground and deposits them into the recycling bin.

Next, Emma watches her grandfather take a third small stone from his right pocket and drop it into his left.

"Why do you carry stones in your pockets?" Emma asks finally, crinkling her eyebrows.

"Oh! But these are no ordinary stones. These are my generosity gems," says Grandpa Phil as he slips his hand into his pocket and pulls out all three stones.

"My gems remind me that every day brings new opportunities to do things for others.

The grey one reminds me to share with a person.

The brown one reminds me to help an animal.

And the white one reminds me to take care of the environment.

Every day, I do my best to make them travel from my right pocket into my left with three acts of kindness."

When they return home,

Emma goes to her bedroom to get her treasure box,

where she keeps her bead collection.

After choosing a purple, a pink and a green bead, she drops them into the right pocket of her overalls.

First, Emma walks around her house and turns off all the lights that do not need to be on.

Plop! goes the pink bead into her left pocket.

Next, Emma cleans
Jellybean's litter box
without even being asked.

plop!
goes the purple
bead into her left pocket.

Finally, Emma places her favourite teddy bear on her brother's pillow.

Plop! goes the green bead into her left pocket.

That night before bed, Emma drops a few more coins into her pockets so she can make them chime by hopping around like a kangaroo.

Then she slips her three generosity gems back into her right pocket.

Now she is ready for tomorrow, just like Grandpa Phil!